The Little PANDA and his BLUE FEET

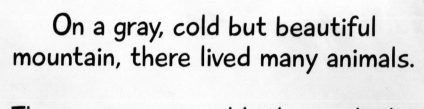

On a gray, cold but beautiful mountain, there lived many animals.

There was a special little panda, he was a little different from all the other animals.

His name was Max, the little panda.

Try me :)

Max was black and white like all pandas were, except he had blue feet.

Because of his blue feet, the other animals would call him "blue foot."

Sometimes, that made him feel sad and alone.

Max's feet would draw attention wherever he would go but not always the right attention.

"Hello little blue foot. Where are your real feet?" said the wolf.

Max looked at his front paws and didn't know what to say.

"Has the cat got your tongue?" the wolf continued.

His feet were real and he hadn't met any cat who wanted to take his tongue.

Max tried to ignore the wolf; he looked down at his feet and continued on his way.

As Max journeyed across the mountain, he encountered a rabbit.

"Hi there blue foot, did you step in some paint? Hahaha...," the rabbit teased, laughing as he bounced away.

Soon afterwards, Max met two leopards.

"Look at his feet," said one leopard to the other.

"A prize to whoever finds the blue foot's lost black socks," quipped the second leopard.

Suddenly, Max decided he needed to run away.

He liked to run usually, but this time he just wanted to be somewhere else, so he ran.

He ran as fast as his feet would allow.

Max was sad to hear the animals only ever talking about his blue feet.

Not having black feet like the other pandas was not his choice. Maybe, he could change his feet.

After a while Max came up with a plan.

To end the jokes, he decided to look for a way to cover his feet, something so the other animals wouldn't notice the blue.

But how could he do it?

Max climbed higher up the mountain to a place where he knew a tree burned last summer.

Max brushed the snow off the tree trunk and rubbed some ash all over his four paws.

It worked! He had to use all of the ash, but his feet were completely black.

Several animals happened to run past him; they didn't notice his feet which meant no blue jokes.

And he was happy for a moment.

He felt like running with the animals.

But, Max realized there was a problem. He could not run, and running was his favorite thing to do!

Because if he did, the ash would fall away, revealing his blue feet again.

"What is the point of having black feet if I can't run!" Max complained to himself.

His happiness faded away again.

Max let out a sigh and decided that trying to be the same as other animals was too hard.

He felt like he should leave
the mountain.

So, he ran.

If his blue feet couldn't let him be happy, then they could at least let him be alone.

He stopped after some time, exhausted, and lay under a big tree next to a beautiful lake.

Max cried himself to sleep.

After some time, he awoke. The night was quiet, and as he gazed out at the moonlight shining across the lake's surface, he suddenly saw the outline of a deer who was taking a drink of water from the lake.

The deer looked up at Max.

"Excuse me little panda, I didn't see you there. This is my favorite place to take a fresh drink, but usually I'm here all by myself," said the deer. "You are welcome to join me."

Max was surprised that the deer called him "'little panda'" and didn't call him "'blue foo!t!

"Pardon me deer, but you might not be seeing me right. I think I am not really a panda," said Max, looking at his feet.

"Well, if not a panda, then what are you?" asked the deer, just as confused as Max.

"As you can see, I don't have black feet like all pandas do, I have blue feet, and as all the animals tell me, that makes me a "blue foot."

"'Blue foot' did you say?" asked the deer. "Well, that's just one part of you. And if I can see you right in this moonlight, I can see you have a panda's body, you have soft fur and a little cute nose, like every other panda."

Max looked up at the deer.

"Even at night, I can see your ears and your paws are shaped like those of all pandas," said the deer, while casually chewing on some leaves.

"I can see I have paws that are shaped like other pandas and if I look at myself in the lake, I can see my ears and nose, but when I see myself in the words of other animals, the only thing I see are my blue feet."

"The truth must be that I am different," said Max.

"Of course you are, you are really different!" cried the deer. "But who is not? And who would not want to be different? We all have something that makes us unique."

"Do you see my left antler, it's longer than my right antler, and longer than most other deers' antlers," said the deer. "It's so long I can scratch my own back with it!"

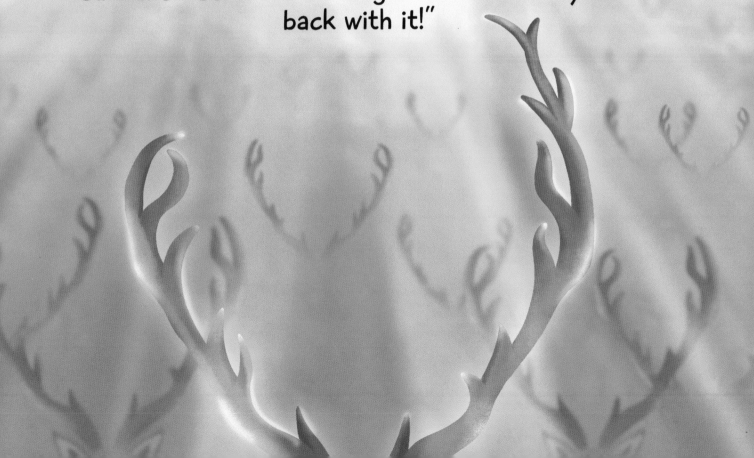

"Being different makes me sad. Don't you ever feel sad about your antler?" asked Max.

"Why would I feel sad? Although they're part of me, my antlers don't make me less of a deer, just as your blue feet don't make you less of a panda," said the deer.

"Over time, I learned to see that being unique is a good thing, worth celebrating and can make you happy!"

Max looked at his feet again and sighed.
"But they're so blue!"

"Little blue foot, what is your name?"
asked the deer.

"It's Max. No one really ever stops to
ask me that," replied Max.

"Nice to meet you, Max," said the deer.
"I'm Sam."

"Max, although we are mostly like our friends, if we look closer, we all have something different.

"Your blue feet do make you different, it's true, but differences can lift you up if you allow them, and that's something worth cherishing.

"Your differences are worth more than everyone else's sameness combined."

And so it was, on a beautiful moonlit night, Max met a great friend who helped him recognize and appreciate differences.

Sam helped Max see what really matters in life, values such as kindness, understanding and friendship,

and most importantly, to love who you are.